Gallant Women: Stories From Kargil

by

Shruti Surendra Nishad

Double9 BOOKS

Gallant Women: Stories From Kargil

by Shruti Surendra Nishad

ISBN: 978-93-67140-31-4

Published by

DOUBLE 9 BOOKS

2/13-B, Ansari Road
Daryaganj, New Delhi – 110002
info@double9books.com
www.double9books.com
Tel. 011-40042856

ABOUT THE AUTHOR

Shruti Surendra Nishad is an enthusiastic writer dedicated to sharing information and inspiring young readers through her book. With a profound interest in military history, she embarked on a mission to uncover the remarkable contributions of women during the Kargil War. Through her book "Gallant Women: Stories from Kargil," she aims to inspire young readers with the courageous narratives of these unsung heroes, highlighting their pivotal roles in the history of India. Shruti meticulously emphasizes the strength, resilience, and determination of these women in the face of adversity. Her passion for storytelling and commitment to honoring these remarkable figures make “Gallant Women” a compelling read that not only educates but also empowers readers to recognize the significant yet often overlooked contributions of women in times of conflict. Her work serves as a powerful reminder that heroism and sacrifice extend beyond the battlefield, enriching our understanding of true valor.

CONTENTS

DEDICATED TO,

The Brave women who served during the Kargil War your courage resilience and unwavering spirit are testament to the strength of humanity. This book is dedicated to you and all the women who served in the armed force medical field and media of often in a face of great danger.

May your stories inspire generations.

FORWARD

In the annals of military history, the voice and contribution of women often stand in the shadow of their male counterparts. The kargil war of 1999 was no exception, yet alchemist the valor of soldiers on a front line there were remarkable women whose courage and resilience shaped the course of history. Galant woman stories from kargil is a tribute to these unsung heroes whose stories deserve to be told and celebrated.

Through the page of this book it uncovered the narrative of women like Gunjan Saxena and the flight Lieutenant Srividya Rajan, who defined norms and flew into the heart of conflict, risking their life to evacuate the wounded and support there comrades. We honour Caption DR. Seema Rao, India's first woman commando trainer, who's dedication to preparing soldiers for the rigors of combat remains unparalleled.

This book is not just about their action during those tumultuous days but also about the resigns of medical personal and nurses who worked tirelessly to save life amidst chaos. It's about the journalists who brought the reality of War to our door step, often facing danger themselves. It's about the families whose to strong on the home front supporting their loved one with unwavering faith and resolve.

PREFACE

In the summer of 1999, the Kargil war brought to the forefront the valor and sacrifice of many unsung heroes. While the world watched the unfolding conflict, a group of exceptional women stabbed into rules that were as critical as they were perilous. "Gallant Women: Stories From Kargil" is it tribute to these women – warriors, healers and chronicles - who displayed extraordinary courage and dedication in a face of adversity.

This book delves into the life of female pilots who flew daring mission, doctors and nurses who saved countless life under fire, and journalist who brought the realities of War to the public. The stories are not just tales of duty but of unwavering resolve and indomitable sprit.

Among these gallant women are Captain DR. Seema Rao, who provided critical medical care on a front lines; Gunjan Saxena and Flight Lieutenant Srividya Rajan, who navigated treacherous skies to evacuate the wounded; and Bharka Datt, whose fearless reporting from the world zone kept the nation informed.

Their contribution are pivotal in shape in the outcomes of the war and serve as a powerful remainder of the strength and resilience women bring to every field. This book aim to honour there legacy and inspire future generation to recognize and celebrate the vital roles women play in our society.

As you read through this compelling narratives, I hope you will be moved by their courage and inspired by their dedication. "Gallant Women: Stories From Kargil" is a testament to the heroism that often goes unnoticed but deserves to be remembered and celebrated.

ACKNOWLEDGMENTS

Writing "Gallant Women: Stories From Kargil" has been a profound journey, and I am deeply great full to all those who have supported me.

First and foremost, I extend my grate full thanks to the brave women whose stories grace this pages .courage and dedication are the heart of this book.

A special thank to the historians, military personnel, and researchers who provided the necessary context and background for these stories. Their expertise and knowledge were crucial in bringing this book to life.

To my family, friends and teachers, thank you for your unwavering support and encouragement. Your believe in me keep me going through the challenging movements.

I would also like to acknowledge my publication whose meticulous attention to detail and insightful feedback helped shape this book into its final form.

Finally to all the readers, thank you for taking the time to engage with this stories. It is my hope that "Gallant Women: Stories From Kargil" will inspire you and honour the incredible contribution of these women.

With sincere gratitude,

Shruti Surendra Nishad

PROLOGUE

The Kargil war of 1999 was a defining movement in India's military history. As the nation grappled with the sudden incursion, a wave of patriotism and unity swept across the country. Among those who wrote to the challenge where a group of extraordinary woman whose contributions, though often overshadowed, where instrument tell in the war effort.

This book "Gallant Women: Stories From Kargil" is a homemade to this unsung heroes. It aims to bring to light the stories of female pilots who braved enemy fire, medical professionals who saved lives under the most challenging condition and journalist who risked everything to report from the front lines.

Through their narrative, the glimpse not just the war's tactical and strategic dimensions but also the human spirit's resilience and strength. These women defined traditional rules and broke barriers, proving there mettle in rules traditionally dominated by men. The stories are a testament to courage, determination and unwavering belief in their mission.

I
INTRODUCTION

" Strength lies not just in physical Power, but in the correct to upload our Nations on our and defend it against all odds."

- Captain Vijayant Thappar

In the spring of 1999, the serene mountainous region of kargil, nestled in the Northern part of Jammu and Kashmir, become the unexpected theater of one of the most significant conflicts between India and Pakistan since their independence. The Kargil war also known as a Kargil conflict , begin when Pakistani infiltrators, added by Pakistan's army, occupied strategic position along the Line of Control (LOC).

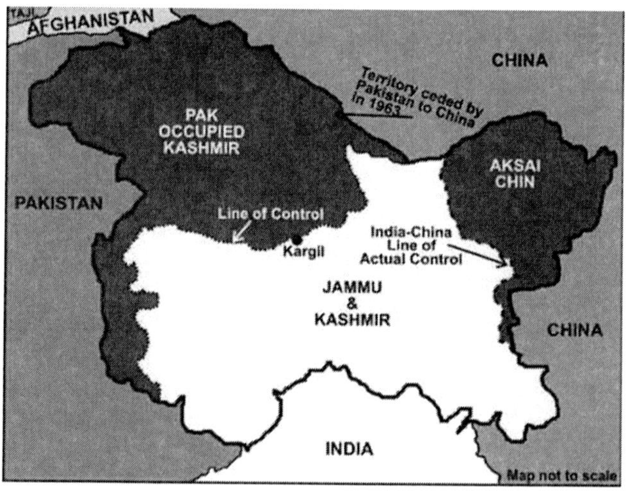

Image by INDIAN TODAY

The origin of the conflict can be traced back to long standing territorial dispute and tension between India and Pakistan over the reason of Kashmir. The Pakistani forces, under the guise of local militants, strategically seized key vantage points terrain off Kargil including heights such as such as Tiger hill, Tololing point, 4845 (also known as Batalik) and other.

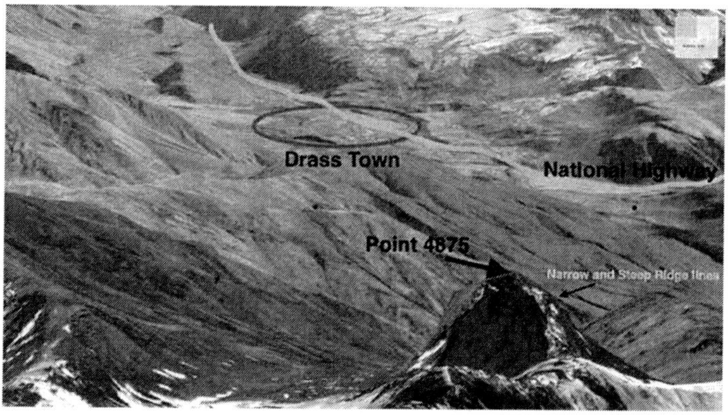

Brass town, Tololing, point 4875(also known as Batalik), National Highway.

These heights overlooked crucial supply routes and Roads leading to the strategic town of Kargil and beyond posing a direct threat Indian military and civilian assets in the region. The infiltration and occupation of these heights Pakistani forces violated the sanctity of the line is control and posed a grave challenges to Indian sovereignty.

The ensuing conflict saw intense battles fought at high altitudes, with Indian forces, including the Indian army with "Operation Vijay" and the Indian Air force with their Operations "Safed Sagar" and Indian Navy carried out "Operation Talwar", understanding daring operation to evict the entrenched enemy from these formidable position.

The terrain was treacherous, marked by steep cliffs, narrow valleys, and extreme weather, which posed immense challenges to both sides.

Image by defense squad, IAF commenced operation Safed Sagar, 1999 in Kargil sector

Image by udChalo

Amidst this back drop of conflict and valor emerged the stories of gallant women who played crucial roles in supporting the war effort. From medical personnel providing critical care to wounded soldiers in makeshift hospitals, to journalist risking their lives to report from the frontline, these Women displayed extraordinary courage and resilience in the face of adversity.

"Gallant women: Stories From Kargil" is a tribute to these unsung heroes, whose contributions and sacrifices during those tumultuous days in the kargil region remains etched in the annals of history. Their stories, alongside those of the brave soldiers who fought for their nation's honor, serve as a testament to the indomitable spirit and unity of purpose that prevailed during the Kargil War.

II
PIONEERS IN ACTION

"A soldier's greatest weapon is courage, not his gun"

- Captain Vikram Batra

In the annals of military history, the kargil war of 1999 stands as testament to the indomitable spirit and valiant efforts of the Indian armed forces. Among the many heroes of this conflict were women who shattered stereotypes, defined societal norms, and demonstrated extraordinary courage and resilience. These pioneers in action played crucial roles that were pivotal to the success of India's military operations in the rugged terrain of kargil.

"I was clear that when I don the uniform, I am on par with my male counterparts, and I must do everything to maintain that respect."

1. Flight Lieutenant Gunjan Saxena:

As one of the first Women to fly into combat zone flight, Lieutenant Gunjan Saxena made history during the Kargil war. Serving as a pilot in the Indian Air force, Gunjan Saxena flew helicopter in hazardous condition, providing critical supplies to troops and evacuating wounded soldiers from the battlefield. Her fearless approach and unwavering commitment earned her the moniker "Kargil Girl" and her story continues to inspire countless young women to pursue careers in the armed force. For her exemplary service, she was awarded the "SHAURYA CHAKRA" award.

Flight Lieutenant Gunjan Saxena got selected in the Indian Air Force along with 25 other women trainee pilots in the year 1994. This was the first batch of women IAF trainee pilots. She was posted in Udhampur, Jammu and Kashmir.

During the Kargil War between India and Pakistan in 1999, Gunjan along with her fellow lieutenant Srividya Rajan got an opportunity to serve the nation. Indian Army carried out two major operations during Kargil War—Operation Vijay and Operation Safed Sagar. Flight Lieutenant Gunjan Saxena was associated with Operation Vijay. She was tasked to evacuate injured soldiers, surveillance of Pakistani soldiers' positions in the war zone and suppling crucial types of equipment to the Indian army units at Dras and Batalik sectors.

In an interview, Gunjan Saxena stated that she had to face Pakistani gunfire and missiles while evacuating the injured soldiers from the war zone.

Women in the 19th century were not allowed to fly in the war zone due to the extreme physical and mental pressure but at the time of Kargil War, India desperately needed all the pilots to attain victory in Pakistan. Thus, all male and female pilots were called in to serve the nation.

Her journey was not without Its challenges, as she often faced skepticism and bias in a predominantly male profession. However, Saxena's determination and skill silenced her critics and paved the way for future generations of female aviators. Her legacy is a testament to the power of perseverance and the importance of breaking barriers.

Gunjan Saxena retired from the Indian Air Force in 2004 after serving for several years. Her retirement came after a distinguished career, including her notable role during the Kargil War.After Kargil, I received the "Shaurya Veer" award from a civilian organisation in Uttar Pradesh.

Image by Janam TV english of kargil girl "Gunjan Saxena"

2. Flight Lieutenant Srividya Rajan:

Alongside Gunjan Saxena, Flight Lieutenant Srividya Rajan also played a significant role in the air operations over Kargil. She undertook daring missions to supply frontline troops and evacuate casualties, navigating the treacherous mountains and hostile conditions. Rajan's contributions exemplify the bravery and dedication of women in the Indian Air Force, highlighting their integral role in military operations.For her valor and service, she was also recognized with the Shaurya Chakra.

Flight Lieutenant Srividya Rajan played a significant role in the Kargil War as one of the first female pilots in the Indian Air Force (IAF). She, alongside Flight Lieutenant Gunjan Saxena, was tasked with critical reconnaissance missions in the conflict zone, flying unarmed Cheetah helicopters.

During the Kargil War, the Cheetah helicopter was indispensable due to its high-altitude capabilities. It performed critical tasks such as casualty evacuation, delivering supplies to frontline troops, and conducting reconnaissance missions. Despite the challenging terrain and adverse weather conditions, the Cheetah's agility and reliability were key to successful operations. Pilots, including pioneers like Gunjan Saxena, flew daring missions under enemy fire. The Cheetah's role was crucial in maintaining the logistical and operational efficiency of Indian forces. Its contributions significantly impacted the outcome of the conflict.

Srividya Rajan and Gunjan Saxena's daring missions involved flying at low altitudes to evacuate wounded soldiers and supply troops in Kargil's treacherous terrains. Their work was pivotal in the successful execution of the war strategies. Srividya was instrumental in carrying out reconnaissance and surveillance operations, often under enemy fire. Hailing from Kerala Srividya Rajan was another IAF pilot to fly in a war zone during Kargil War. Srividya was posted at Udhampur in Jammu Kashmir sector.

Srividya Rajan's flights were marked by their perilous nature, as they navigated through the high-altitude conflict zones of Kargil. Her bravery and skill were exemplary, reflecting the growing role of women in the IAF.

Srividya's missions not only demonstrated her flying capabilities but also her courage under extreme conditions.

Srividya Rajan's participation in the Kargil War is noted as a groundbreaking moment for women in the Indian armed forces. Her flights involved strategic reconnaissance and transportation tasks that were crucial for the success of the Indian military operations. Srividya's contributions were a testament to her resolve and skill as a pilot.

These sources collectively emphasize Srividya Rajan's bravery, her critical role in reconnaissance and evacuation missions, and her contributions to the Kargil War, showcasing the expanding role of women in the Indian military.

Flight Lieutenant Srividya Rajan is a retired Indian Air force officer known for her role in a Kargil War, where she was one of the flew women pilot involved in the conflict. She is active as a motivational speaker and shares her experience from the Kargil war and her career in the Air force. She participate in various event and forums focused on women empowerment, defense and aviation.

3. Captain (Dr.) Seema Rao:

Captain (Dr.) Seema Rao, India's first woman commando trainer, and has trained over 15000 commandos in the Indian armed force, brought her expertise to the four front during Kargil conflict. Though not directly involved in combat rigorous training program for Indian commando's ensure that the troops were well prepared for the high altitude warfare the encountered. Dr. Rao's dedication to enhancing the capabilities of India's elite forces underscore the critical support roles women played behind the scenes. Her contributions to command or train in has been widely acknowledged and celebrated.

Captain(Dr.) Seema Rao (first and only women commando trainer)

She is one of the rarest people in a world who have master the art of 'Jeet Kone Do' (It is an eclectic and hybrid martial art founded by Bruce Lee in 1967) and she further God authorised to teach the same. Apart from all the accolades and awards, she has also received: world peace award by world peace Congress, Malaysia award by prime Minister of Malaysia for contribution to the country in 2008, us president's volunteer service award, three army Chief Citation, home minister of India letter of Commendation in 2009 placing on record the selfless nation service in the field of close quarters battle training, and a 1000 facilitation from Indian Government.

Fighting it out against all odds, in a male dominated field of commando training, she wants revealed how some people she started training showd displeasure on being trained by women commander. In an interview with Naree, Seema said;

"Not only did I have to discipline them, but I also had to gain their confidence in my ability to teach. However, eventually I have always manage to earn the respect of commandos that I have trained."

Captain (Dr.) Seema Rao, India's first female commander trainer, play the significant role during the Kargil war and has contributed extensively to India's defense forces. Dr. Rao and her husband also trained various police forces in urban counter terrorism tactics, which particularly crucial following the 2008 Mumbai attacks. Dr. Rao's work has inspired many and he continuous to be a motivational speaker, sharing her journey and empowering others, specially women to achieve their full potential.

Dr. Seema Rao's unwavering commitment to training Indian defence force and her innovative approaches to combat training have made her and invaluable asset to the nation. Her story is one of resilience, dedication and significant impact on a India security landscape.

Captain (Dr.) Seema Rao, a prominent figure in Indian military history and a trailblazer in women's empowerment, has received the several award and recognitions for her contributions.

1. Shaurya chakra: India's third highest peas time military decoration.
2. President police medal for Meritorious Service: award for her exceptional Service.
3. Sena medal: military honour for distinguished service
4. National women's award: Recognizes her role in promoting women's empowerment.
5. India's top 50 most powerful women: Recognized by various organizations for her influence and impact.

She has also been acknowledged in various other forums for her significant contribution to the Indian army and her efforts in promoting women in defence and martial arts.

4. Major Priya Jhingan:

As one of the first woman to join the Indian army, major Priya jingle paved the way for future generation of female officer. During the Kargil war her leadership and organizational skills were instrumental in managing logistic and support for the troops. A decade ago, on 21st September 1992, the feisty Priya Jhingan Android as 001- the first lady cadet to join the Indian army. "It's a dream I have to lived everyday for the last 10 years," says Jhingan, formerly OIC, Judge Advocate. Major Jhingan's trailblazing journey in the army inspired many young women to follow in her foot steps, breaking barriers in predominantly male dominated field.

In February 2018, Major Priya Jhingan was felicitated by the president of India, Shri Ram Nath Kovind, for being the pioneer of women in the Indian army amongst 112 other prominent women in various field in India.

Priya Jhingan was one of the first woman to be Commissioned into the Indian army. During the Kargil War, she was serving with a military nursing service (MNS). Her roll primarily involved providing critical medical support in the battlefield, where she was responsible for treating injured Soldier and managing medical logistic under challenging condition.

Knowing for her bravery and leadership, Jhingan exhibited exceptional commitment under the harsh condition of the war. She was actively involved in both field and hospital setting, managing the health care need of troops in high pressure environment.

Major Priya Jhingan

Dedication and service during the Kargil war and her recognition from both her peers and the military establishment. She become a symbol of the critical role women play in military operations, demonstrating that air contribution are invaluable and indispensable.

She was awarded the Silver Medal during the passing out parade at the academic on 6th March 1993. In March 1993, Priya become the first woman to be Commissioned into the Judge Advocate Journal's Department of the Indian army. She topped the Young Officers course and was awarded and 'Instructor Grading'.

5. Captain Ruchi Sharma:

Another trailblazing figure is Captain Ruchi Sharma, an officer in a Indian Army Signals Corps. Captain Sharma went on to be called as 'India's first female operational paratooper.' Sharma is a daughter of an Indian Army Officer and both of them are the alumni of the Officer's Training Academy, Chennai. During the Kargil conflict captain Sharma was entrusted with the crucial task of maintaining communication lines, ensuring seamless connectivity for the troops deployed in the rugged terrains. Despite facing numerous challenges and a constant threat of enemy attack, she carried out her duty with unmatched dedication cation and efficiency.

For her exemplary service, Captain Ruchi Sharma what awarded the Sena Medal, one of the India's highest military honour. This recognition was a testament to her bravery and the critical nature of her contribution during war.

Captain Ruchi Sharma join the army 1996 and qualified to become the first woman operation Paratrooper. *A Paratrooper is a military parachutist friend to jump from planes using a parachute to land at a designated spot.* Paratrooper are often used in surprise attack during war.

Captain Ruchi Sharma, who quit in 2003, leapt of an aircraft some 10 year ago to become the first operational women Paratrooper. *" Paratrooper have an aura of their own. I always dream of breaking into this league of extraordinary gentleman." She said.* Ruchi Sharma, one of the 350 women who have literally change the face of Indian Army, is the daughter of an army officer who passed out from the same Officer's Training Academy in Chennai that has daughter did. With her maroon beret at a rakish angle, proudly notice that she is a professional paratooper not a recreational one.

In an interview of Femina magazine she remember that during training they were made to jog for 40 km with a 10 kg load. Her first jump was in 1997. About her first jump she say, "The first jump is like your first love."; in an Indian express article she is quoted saying, "I was screaming my parent's names, telling them that I love them," and adding, "but when I landed, my 'ustad' burst my bubble saying the enemy will know my position if I screamed so much every time I jumped." I Sharma went on to on the maroon beret and serve in area such as Ladakh.

"We fought not for glory, but for the honour of the nation."

Captain Ruchi Sharma

Picking about her professional, the officer who belong to a league of 350 women who literally change the face of Indian Defense Force, said: " Paratrooper have their aura of their own. I always dreamed to breaking into this league of extraordinary gentleman." The retired para officer further said: "I think women should be given a chance to take a combat arms. I am not even saying man and woman have equal physical strength. Having women will result in a good, healthy institution."

Does the stories of this pioneering women in action during the Kargil war are a testament to their bravery, resilience and unwavering commitment to their country. Their contribution, weather in the Skies, on the ground, or behind the scenes where crucial to the success of India's military efforts. As we honor these Gallant Women, very good nice your legacy of breaking barrier and inspiring future generation to serve with courage and dedication.

III
HEALING HANDS

"in the battlefield, the courage of a soldier is bolstered not just by the weapon he carries, but why the assurance that someone will be there to tend two his wounds and left his spirits. Our medical teams are the true unsung heroes."

- Lieutenant General Yogesh Kumar Joshi

The Kargil war of 1999 stand as a testament to the valor and resilience of the Indian Armed Forces. Amidst the fierce battles and strategic maneuver, there emerged a group of unsung heroes whose contribution where critical yet often over shadowed by the Chaos of War.

There were the women in medical and nursing roll who's healing hand brought solace and recovery to the wounded Soldier. Beyond the officers in a limelight, countless other woman served in various capacities during the Kargil War, showcasing their versatility and determination. From nursing wounded Soldier to provide in crucial intelligence and logistical support, their contribution where invaluable in and sharing the success of military operation.

Captain (Dr.)Seema Roy, one of the prominent figure in a medical cops during the Kargil conflict , she known as a India first woman commando trainer, she also served on a front line, providing essential medical care under challenging condition. Her patient not only boost at the moral of the troops but also underscored the critical role of medical professionals in combat zone.

The unsung heroines of nursing while doctor like Captain Rao where at the four front, the nurses working tirelessly Enfield hospitals played an equally vital roles. These women, after working round the clock, standard to the injured soldiers with compassion and expertise.

There work all the less visible, was low less heroic. They faced the same risk as the soldiers, dealing with the constant threat of enemy fire and the horse condition of the mountainous terrain.

Stories of dedication Flight Lieutenant Srividya Rajan, alongside Flight Lieutenant Gunjan Saxena, become one of the first woman to fly into a combat zone, evacuating the wounded and bringing them to safely. The courage under fire and determination to save life become a beacon of hope for many.

"In her interviews, Gunjan Saxena after recounts the harrowing ear full film experience of serving during the Kargil War. Every time I flew , I knew I was helping save a life. It was my duty and my honour," she said in her interviews.

The role of women in medical logistics and sure that surprise where adequately stopped and distributed. These included everything from surgical instrument to essential medications. There efficiency in managing the supplies was critical in maintaining the functionality of field hospitals.

Nursing officer, after the unsung heroes, play a pivotal role in patient care and recovery. The duties range from assisting in surgeries to providing post operative care and emotional support. In " Letters from Kargil: The War Through Our Soldier's Eyes" by Diksha Dwivedi, several letters from soldiers mansion the compassion and care the received from the nursing staff, emphasizing the cycle logical come for provided by these dedicated professionals.

The Psychological Impact: the cycle logical tool of War is immense, and the medical staff often provided not just physical but emotional support to the soldier. The ability to offer a kind word, a reassuring smile or simply a comforting presence in times of distress was invaluable.

Many soldiers have spoken about how the care and empathy of these women help them through their darkest hour. Apart from physical injuries, psychological impact of War required attention. Medical professionals were trained to recognize and treat combat stress and trauma. "Victory in Kargil" by kernel Anil Shorey discusses the integration of psychological support within the medical units highlighting the holistic approach to soldiers care.

The medical professionals of the Kargil War exemplified courage, innovation and compassion. The stories of bravery and dedication continue to inspire, highlighting the critical role of medical support in war time. As we remember the heroes of Kargil, the healing hand that tended to the wounded hold a special place ace in our heart and history.

These unsung heroes, after working under extreme condition, demonstrated an unwavering commitment to their duty. The relentless noise of artillery fire, the harsh weather condition and the constant rate of enemy attack did not deter them from their mission. Their resilience in the face of adversity provided a beacon of hope and strength to the soldiers they treated.

Medical staff during Kargil War

Furthermore, the medical staff ability to adapt to rapidly, changing situation was nothing short of remarkable. Day after had to make quick decisions with limited resources, employing their skills and ingenuity to save lives. Stories of make shift operating theatres and innovative medical procedures during the Kargil war are a testament to their resourcefulness and determination.

The impact of their effort extends beyond the battlefield. Many soldiers to returned home carried with them not just physical scars but also the emotional resilience imported by these compassionate caregiver. The bond between the medical staff and the soldiers the treated is a poignant reminder of the profound human connection forged in times of conflict.

In commemoration the Kargil war it is essential to honour not just as soldiers who fought on the front line but also those who worked tirelessly behind the scenes. Their contribution were crucial in ensuring the well being and recovery of the troops and there legacy continues to inspire new generation of medical professionals in the armed force.

Reflecting on her experience Barkha Dutt, a journalist who cover the Kargil war extensively wrote, "The nurses and doctors where the unsung heroes of kargil. Their unwavering dedication and resilience under fire were nothing short of extraordinary."

Dr. Seema Rao, in her memories noted, "In the midst of War, it was the small act of kindness and the unwavering spirit of my colleagues that keep us going. The side of a soldiers recovery was the greatest reward we could ask for."

The story of Dr. Arup Basu in the Kargil War

Dr. Arup during the Kargil was is a testament to dedication and Resilience. In the year of 1999 as the Kargil conflict erupted in the rugged mountains of Jammu and Kashmir, Dr. Arup Basu was stationed at a military hospital. The surgery is would start at about 8:30 p.m. -9:30 p.m. and continue throughout the night. A seasoned medical professional he was no stranger to the challenges of providing medical care in the conflict zones, birthday Kargil war presented a new set of obstacles. The high altitude, treacherous terrain, and relentless enemy fire made every task a test of endurance an ingenuity.

Dr. Basu vividly recalls the day he received orders to move closer to the front lines. The gravity of the situation was clear—Indian soldiers were engaged in fierce battles to reclaim territory, and casualties were mounting. As he prepared to leave, thoughts of his family flickered in his mind, but his resolve to serve his country overshadowed any personal fears.

Upon arriving at the makeshift field hospital near the front lines, Dr. Basu was immediately struck by the dire conditions. The hospital, a collection of tents and temporary structures, was constantly under threat from enemy shelling. Supplies were limited, and the high altitude made every physical effort more exhausting. Despite these challenges, Dr. Basu and his team got to work.

The wounded began arriving in droves. Many had sustained severe injuries from shrapnel and gunfire, while others suffered from altitude sickness and frostbite. Dr. Basu's experience and leadership were crucial in organizing the chaotic influx of patients. He quickly established triage protocols to prioritize the most critical cases and devised innovative medical techniques to address the unique injuries caused by high-altitude warfare.

One of Dr. Basu's most vivid memories from the war is the relentless focus required to perform life-saving surgeries under the constant threat of shelling. *"In the midst of the conflict, our primary objective was to stabilize and treat the wounded soldiers swiftly and efficiently. The harsh terrain and weather added to the complexity of our task, but our commitment to saving lives remained unwavering," he recalls.*

I operated upon 300 soldiers, and lost one, If soldiers came to us as 'brought dead' then the medical officer would certify them. I had certified the mortal remains of martyr Squadron Leader Ajay Ahuja who was killed by the Pakistanis, he said.

Image: Dr Arup Basu, sitting second from left, and the medical staff at a military hospital in Kargil during the 1999 war

In June the multilated body of captain Saurabh Kalia and his patrol where return to them. On hearing about the extreme injuries inflicted on them, the same soldiers wear appeared extremely despondent in the field hospital was suddenly transform the into a burning dynamite.

The soldiers used to tell him that you have to make us recover fast because they want to get back to the battlefield and avenge their deaths. 'We will get to eat and everyone of them they would say. And then the war turned. The soldier started capturing peak after peak – Tololing, Peak 4875, Tiger hill and Batalik ridges.

Battle of Tololing (13th JUNE)

DR . Basu's role extended beyond medical treatment. He also coordinate it the evacuation of critically injured soldiers, after under dangerous conditions. The use of helicopters for medical evacuation was crucial, but the risk of being targeted by enemy fire made every mission perilous. Dr. Basu's meticulous planning and clam demeanor during these evaluation were instrumental in saving countless lives.

The psychological toll of the war was immense. Many soldiers grappled with the trauma of combat, and Dr. Basu recognized the importance of addressing their mental health. He and his team provided psychological support, helping soldiers cops with the horrors of battle and maintain their morale.

The contribution of these women extend beyond their immediate impact during the Kargil War. They have inspired complex other to pursue career in medical field within the military. Their stories as a powerful remainder of a vital role women play in our armed forces, not just as combatants but as healer and caregivers.

As we honor the heroes of kargil, let us not forget the healing hand that work tirelessly behind the scenes. Their dedication, bravery and compassion have left an indelible mark on the history of the Indian Armed Forces, inspiring future generation to serve with the spirit and commitment.

The medical professionals of the Kargil War amplified courage, innovation and compassion. Their stories of bravery and dedication continue to inspire, highlight in the critical role of medical support in war time. As we remember the heroes of Kargil, the healing hand that tended to the wounded hold a special place in our heart and history.

IV
JOURNALISTS ON THE FRONTLINE

"Journalists where our voice to the world, bringing the story of our bravery and sacrifices to every home"

- General Ved Prakash Malik

(Former Chief Of Army Staff during the Kargil War)

Journalists play a crucial role in war zones, acting as the eyes and ears of the world. Their reporting brings the harsh realities of conflict to the public, providing a vital service by informing and shaping public opinion. The Kargil War was no exception, with several journalists braving the dangers to cover the conflict from the front lines.

The media are described as the citizens' window to the world because whenever any situation arises, the whole nation looks up to journalists to know what is happening. This role becomes even more prominent during crises and war.

Barkha Dutt is an award-winning TV journalist, anchor and columnist with more than two decades of reporting experience. She is India's only Emmy-nominated journalist who has won multiple national and international awards, including the **Padmashri**, which is India's fourth highest civilian honour.

Barkha Dutt reporting on kargil war

Ms. Dutt graduated from St. Stephen's College, Delhi with a degree in English Literature. She did her Master's in Journalism from the Graduate School of Journalism at Columbia University in New York.

Ms. Dutt has reported from some of the toughest spots and conflict zones in India and across the world including Pakistan, Iraq, Afghanistan, Libya and Egypt. Her frontline reporting of the Kargil war first made her a household name. Dutt began her career at NDTV, where she quickly made a name for herself as a fearless reporter.

Dutt's reporting from the Kargil front lines was groundbreaking. She brought the war into the living rooms of millions, providing not just news but also a human perspective on the conflict. Her interviews with soldiers and their families highlighted the personal sacrifices and stories of bravery that are often overshadowed by the larger narrative of war.

Barkha Dutt's coverage had a profound impact on journalism in India. She inspired a new generation of journalists and brought attention to the role of women in media. Her work during the Kargil War remains a benchmark for war reporting in India.

The Indian media created awareness regarding the Kargil War among the public through their visual impact. They aroused nationalistic fervor and created awareness regarding the hardships faced by the Indian Army.

In India, The Kargil war of 1999 is Nation's first war on television, in fact, it was the first 'live' war of the South Asian region. The Kargil War was fought by the Indian Army with Pakistani infiltrators. The war occurred at a time when electronic media in India was just introduced. This enabled the war to be telecast live across the nation.

According to senior journalist VC Natrajan "the press had access to forward areas when the war broke out. Neither the top brass of the armed forces nor the bureaucracy made any effort to hinder the media from reporting what was happening on the battlefront."

There were also blunders like the blazing lights of cameramen outside the Brigade Headquarters at Drass drew the attention of the enemy which led to heavy shelling in which four soldiers were killed and the correspondent of a national daily was injured.

Every reporter during their academic years have read about the Basic Journalism Ethics, which teaches how a moral media person should report, it also helps journalists. In collecting and disseminating news by ensuring objectivity and fairness in reporting information to society. Similarly, in a war-like situation, the role of 'Journalism Ethics' becomes more prominent and critical otherwise, the reporter may end up leaking sensitive information about the country that can prove fatal to national security as journalist" Barkha Dutt did during the Kargil war.

No one can forget how her dubious Kargil coverage spooked the army during the Kargil war, from providing crucial information about the secret operation to reviling military locations.

The Kargil War was fought between the Indian Army and the Pakistan Army in the Kargil region between May and July 1999. Since the war took place at a time when India's electronic media was just getting started, the media began providing more detailed media coverage of the Kargil war. Media outlets, like NDTV, and Star News channels had even started telecasting war footage live on TV to gain more TRP. Soon, the conflict became the first "live" war in South Asia even Major General Ashok Mehta also called it, "India's first war on television."

Barkha Dutt was one of the journalists who was covering the "live war' for NDTV. She gained prominence for irresponsibly doing a live commentary during the "secret" Tiger Hill operation. While covering the operation, Barkha Dutt gave away the military location by concluding her live commentary by saying "Barkha Dutt reporting from 56 Brigade HQ" at the end.

Besides *Lt Gen Mohinder Puri in his book 'Kargil: Turning the Tide'* (page no. 92)said that the army might have got unnerved because of journalist Barkha Dutt's irresponsible journalism.

It reads, "At about 2120 hours, the exchange operator gave a ring in the ops room asking for me. The Corps Commander wanted to speak to me urgently. When the call got connected, all in the ops room could make out that something serious was being discussed between us. On finishing, I looked at Col SVE David, Deputy Cdr of 56 Mtn Bde, who was also present, and asked him to find out if Barkha Dutt of NDTV, then Star Plus/News Channel, was anywhere in the vicinity or amongst the media witnessing the artillery fire on Tiger Hill.

Lt. Gen. Mohinder Puri

We soon discovered that the young lady was giving a live commentary on the attack on Tiger Hill sitting right next to the brigade traffic check post in Drass. I met her and after a few words of advice from me, she was told to proceed to an underground room and rest for the night. So much for the secrecy of an operation! I had only informed the Corps Cdr of the date of the operation and he in turn for reasons of secrecy had not even informed the Army Cdr. Hence the surprise and concern over Barkha's reporting."

Even the then Army chief, General V.P Malik, who led the army in 1999 during the Kargil war, had specifically quoted in his book (Kargil: From surprise to victory) how Barkha Dutt had revealed classified information during her live coverage. He also pointed out how her reporting was threatening to hurt the secrecy of the operations.

"This puts the whole thing in a new perspective. The fact is that all sources verify that BD was the only journalist in the war zone who had a satellite phone. Also, the number of satellite phones with the Indian army was limited to a few senior-most officers who were not in the conflict zone. Therefore, the chances of BD's satphone being the one tracked by the Pakistanis are very high. The errors of commission and omission, of which BD is accused of, are extremely serious.

After the Dy. Brigade Commander at Drass, Colonel David, briefed BD on the progress of the actual assault on Tiger Hill, BD is reported to have gone live immediately. Indian intercepts of Pakistani military messages indicate that the Pakistani rear commanders immediately alerted their troops on top of Tiger Hill to redirect their fire in the direction of the Indian soldiers who were climbing Tiger Hill. About 14-20 of our soldiers were massacred by this deadly fire and died on the ropes they were using to climb their target."*(From book: Kargil from surprise to victory)*

In a veiled statement, without directly taking the name of Barkha Dutt in his book **'MASHKOH: KARGIL AS I SAW IT',** Brigadier Umesh Singh Bawa's who commanded the 17 Jat during the Kargil war in 1999 also pointed out how few reporters gave away the Indian army's position to Pakistan and invited prompted 'counter bombardment by sending live reports via cell phone.

Since that blunder, everyone felt that Kargil's experience would have made the so-called journalist mature about these aspects, however, she again dug her own grave by repeating the same mistake during the Mumbai 26/11 terror attack.

Interestingly, the Supreme Court too agreed that the media's role during 26/11 was irresponsible and dangerous. Even after such a blunder, that times government of India didn't even take cognizance of the matter. What's more ironic is that a few months after the 26/11 blunder, the Sonia Gandhi-led Manmohan Singh government bestowed the Padma Award 2009 on "Dutt" for her reporting style.

However, recalled Kargil as the most "transformative experience" of her journalistic career, one she considers "a masterclass in life".

The Padma Shri-winning journalist narrated that there was a lot of resistance from the Armed forces to allow her in an "all- male zone" and that she was determined "not to cry one drop of tear" because she had to prove herself "more than the boys".

However one must know the Operational Security (OPSEC) is a key principle in military operations to ensure sensitive information is not disclosed. Critics argue that some of Dutt's reports violated OPSEC guidelines, potentially endangering ongoing military operations.

For instance, her coverage included detailed descriptions of military strategies and troop movements, which are typically kept confidential during active operations.

The controversy surrounding Barkha Dutt's reporting during the Kargil War highlights the complex challenges faced by journalists covering conflict zones. While her work brought important stories to the public, it also underscored the need for responsible journalism that does not compromise operational security. This incident remains a significant case study in the ethics of war reporting, emphasizing the delicate balance between transparency and security.

Challenges Faced by Journalists

1. Covering a war zone is fraught with dangers. Journalists face the risk of being caught in crossfire, shelling, or other military actions. The rugged terrain and harsh weather conditions of the Kargil region added to the difficulties faced by reporters.

2. Getting accurate information during a conflict can be challenging. Journalists often have to rely on military briefings, which may be influenced by propaganda. Balancing the need for timely reporting with the responsibility of accurate and unbiased journalism is a constant challenge.

3. Witnessing the horrors of war can take a significant emotional toll on journalists. They often have to report on the suffering and loss of life while remaining detached enough to do their job effectively. This emotional strain can lead to long-term psychological effects.

The reporting from the Kargil War set new standards for war journalism in India. It highlighted the importance of having journalists on the ground to provide real-time updates and human stories from conflict zones. The bravery and dedication of these journalists ensured that the Kargil War was not just a series of strategic maneuvers but also a human story of courage, sacrifice, and resilience.

Journalists on the front lines of the Kargil War played a pivotal role in shaping public perception and understanding of the conflict. Their courage and commitment to their profession brought the realities of war to the forefront, ensuring that the stories of those who fought and those who suffered were not forgotten. As we remember the Kargil War, we must also honor the journalists who risked their lives to bring us the truth.

V
STRENGTH ON THE HOME FRONT

In the midst of the Kargil War, while soldiers fought valiantly on the battlefield, the strength and resilience of those on the home front were equally pivotal. This chapter explores the stories of women and families who supported the war effort from behind the scenes, their contributions often going unnoticed but profoundly impactful.

These unsung heroes faced their own battles, coping with the anxiety and uncertainty that shadowed their daily lives. Mothers, wives, sisters, and daughters found courage in each other, forming a network of support that uplifted entire communities. They organized supply drives, stitched uniforms, and wrote letters of encouragement that provided much-needed morale boosts to the soldiers far from home.

Among them was Meera, a young woman whose husband was on the front lines. Every day, she visited the local community center, where she and other women gathered to prepare care packages. These packages, filled with homemade snacks, warm clothing, and heartfelt notes, were sent to the soldiers to remind them of the love and gratitude waiting for them back home.

Then there was Asha, a school teacher who took it upon herself to educate the children about patriotism and the sacrifices being made by their families. She organized plays and storytelling sessions, instilling a sense of pride and responsibility in the young minds, ensuring that the legacy of bravery and selflessness would continue through generations.

These women also found solace in traditional rituals and prayers, finding strength in their faith and cultural heritage. They held candlelight vigils and community prayers, creating a sense of unity and purpose that transcended the fear and sorrow of war. Their resilience was not just in enduring the absence of their loved ones but in actively contributing to the war effort, displaying an unwavering spirit that was crucial to the nation's morale.

Through their stories, this chapter aims to shed light on the invaluable role of women and families during times of conflict, recognizing their sacrifices and celebrating their indomitable spirit. Their quiet yet powerful contributions remind us that the fabric of a nation's strength is woven not just by those on the front lines but by the countless hearts that beat in solidarity behind them.

Women played a crucial role in maintaining the morale and support structures for soldiers. They managed households, supported families, and kept the nation's spirit high amidst the uncertainty of war.

> *"Behind every soldier, there are families who bear the burden of waiting and worrying. Their strength is the silent support that fuels our bravery." – Priya Kapoor, Author*

Families of soldiers had to navigate the emotional and practical challenges of having loved ones in the conflict. Their stories reveal a different kind of bravery strength to endure and support from afar. The

> *"When your son or husband is fighting miles away, you realize that your own strength is crucial to their fight. Our endurance was their anchor." Anju Sharma, Wife of a Kargil Soldier.*

Women across India volunteered in various capacities to support the war effort. From organizing fundraisers to providing emotional support, their efforts were instrumental in sustaining the war morale.

> *"Volunteering for the war effort was not just about contributing material support; it was about standing together as a nation, showing solidarity in the face of adversity." – Neelam Sharma, Author*

Understanding the psychological impact of the war on both soldiers and their families sheds light on the critical support systems in place during this time. Women often took on the role of emotional caregivers, providing stability and comfort.

> *"The true battle was not just on the front lines but within the hearts and minds of those waiting at home. Providing psychological support was as vital as any logistical operation." – Dr. S. R. Kumar, Psychologist*

Women and families also engaged with media to raise awareness and garner support. Their voices helped shape public perception and encouraged national solidarity.

> *"The media not only reported the war but also became a platform for the voices of those who supported it from the home front. Their stories brought the war closer to the people." – Rajesh Puri, Author*

The strength displayed on the home front during the Kargil War has left a lasting legacy. Many of these women and families continue to support veterans and their causes, contributing to ongoing military and veteran welfare initiatives.

> *"The legacy of Kargil is not just about the battles fought but about the continued support and strength of those who stood behind the soldiers. Their impact resonates in every act of kindness and support today." Suman Mehta, Author*

Some poignant stories from the families of Kargil heroes and heroines that highlight their contributions and sacrifices:

1. *Captain (Dr.) Seema Rao*

Captain (Dr.) Seema Rao's husband, Major General V. K. Rao, has shared touching accounts of her bravery. During the Kargil War, Captain Rao was stationed in challenging high-altitude areas, providing critical medical care to injured soldiers. Her family recounts how she balanced the pressures of war with her commitment to family life. Her husband recalls the long hours she spent on the phone, reassuring family members while managing life-saving medical operations.

Major General V. K. Rao:

"Seema's dedication was beyond compare. She faced the harsh conditions of Kargil with the same resolve and compassion she brought to our family life. Her strength was a beacon for all of us."

Captain (Dr.) Seema Rao with her husband V.K Rao

2. *Flight Lieutenant Gunjan Saxena:*

Gunjan Saxena's father, K.K. Saxena, has spoken about her courage and the pride they felt watching her fly missions over the conflict zone. Despite the risks, Gunjan was determined to contribute to the war effort. Her family shares how her bravery was a source of inspiration not only for them but also for many others. The Saxena family vividly remembers the tension and the pride as they followed news of her missions.

K.K. Saxena:

Gunjan's courage was not just about flying under fire; it was about her unwavering commitment to serve her country. Her valor during Kargil made us incredibly proud and showed the world the strength of women in combat."

3. *Lieutenant Colonel Saurabh Kalia:*

The Kalia family, particularly Lieutenant Colonel Saurabh Kalia's father, M. S. Kalia, has shared the tragic yet heroic story of Saurabh. Captured and brutally tortured by enemy forces, Saurabh's bravery and ultimate sacrifice became a symbol of the extreme hardships faced by soldiers. His family's accounts emphasize his unwavering dedication and the deep sense of loss felt by his loved ones.

M. S. Kalia:

"Saurabh's sacrifice was the ultimate demonstration of bravery. Though his fate was tragic, his spirit and the stories of his courage continue to inspire us and honor his memory."

Lieutenant Colonel Saurabh Kalia with his mother Mrs. Vijaya Kalia and father M.S Kalia

4. *Captain Vikram Batra:*

Captain Vikram Batra's twin brother, Vishal Batra, has often shared how Vikram's fearless leadership during the Kargil War was a source of immense pride. Captain Batra's courageous acts, particularly his famous quote "Yeh Dil Maange More," became legendary. Vishal recounts how their family followed his exploits with both concern and pride, and his sacrifice has left an indelible mark on them.

Vishal Batra:

"Vikram's bravery was not just a personal achievement; it was a testament to the spirit of our nation. His sacrifice has made our family proud and has left a legacy of courage and patriotism."

5. Major Rajesh Adhikari:

Major Rajesh Adhikari's family has shared his story of valor in the face of adversity. Major Adhikari was involved in several crucial operations and was known for his bravery and leadership. His family speaks of the pride they felt in his accomplishments and the emotional strength they drew from his example during and after the war.

Major Rajesh Adhikari's family:

"Rajesh's courage was a source of immense pride for us. His leadership and sacrifice during the Kargil War are remembered not just by our family but by the entire nation. His story continues to inspire and give us strength."

These stories from families provide a personal and emotional perspective on the sacrifices and bravery of the Kargil heroes and heroines, highlighting the profound impact of their contributions both on the battlefield and within their families.

The Kargil War, a defining moment in India's military history, was not only marked by intense combat and strategic maneuvers but also by the extraordinary contributions of individuals and families behind the scenes. The stories of heroes like Captain (Dr.) Seema Rao, Flight Lieutenant Gunjan Saxena, and Lieutenant Colonel Saurabh Kalia, among others, illustrate the diverse forms of courage and dedication displayed during the conflict.

Their heroism on the battlefield and the unwavering support from their families collectively shaped the outcome of the war and provided a deeper understanding of the sacrifices involved. Families of these soldiers, through their resilience and support, played an equally crucial role, ensuring that their loved ones could face the challenges of war with steadfastness and hope.

Reflect on these narratives, it becomes clear that the strength on the home front is a fundamental component of national resilience. The valor of soldiers is matched by the silent bravery of those who support them from afar. These stories remind us that the impact of war extends beyond the battlefield, influencing and shaping the lives of individuals and communities in profound ways.

In recognizing the sacrifices and contributions of both the heroes in uniform and their families, we gain a fuller appreciation of the complexities of war and the enduring spirit of those who contribute to national defense. Their stories are not just historical accounts but are lessons in courage, sacrifice, and the power of collective strength in the face of adversity.

Thus, this chapter underscores the integral role of the home front during the Kargil War, illustrating how the strength and resilience of those behind the scenes were as vital as the heroism displayed on the battlefield.

VI
COURAGE AND RESILIENCE

The Kargil War of 1999 was not merely a conflict of strategic and military significance; it was also a profound testament to the indomitable human spirit and unparalleled valor. While the bravery of the soldiers has been extensively documented and celebrated, the unsung heroes—the women who played crucial and multifaceted roles—deserve an equally prominent spotlight.

This chapter delves into their extraordinary courage and resilience, alongside the exceptional bravery of their male counterparts. From the battlefield to medical tents, and from piloting rescue missions to frontline journalism, their stories collectively narrate a compelling saga of strength, dedication, and breaking barriers. Together, their efforts have left an indelible mark on history, highlighting the profound impact of both men and women who served with unwavering commitment during this pivotal conflict.

Courage refers to the mental or moral strength to confront fear, danger, or adversity. It involves facing challenging situations bravely, despite the potential for harm or failure. Courage is often demonstrated through actions taken under duress or in the presence of fear.

Resilience is the ability to recover quickly from difficulties or setbacks. It involves maintaining flexibility and strength in the face of adversity, bouncing back from challenges, and adapting positively to difficult circumstances. Resilience reflects how well individuals or groups can withstand and overcome stress, hardship, and change.

In essence, courage is about facing and confronting fears or challenges, while resilience is about enduring and recovering from those challenges over time.

1. Courage: The soldiers and women involved in the Kargil War demonstrated immense courage by directly confronting the dangers of combat, navigating treacherous terrains, and undertaking high-risk missions. For instance, female pilots like Gunjan Saxena and medical personnel faced the perils of war while performing their critical roles.

Despite the inherent fear and uncertainty of war, these individuals displayed bravery by continuing their duties under extreme pressure. This courage is reflected in their unwavering commitment and the risks they took to support their comrades.

2. Resilience: The chapter highlights how both male and female participants dealt with the physical and emotional strains of the war. Resilience is evident in their ability to recover from injuries, cope with the trauma of battle, and persist in their roles despite the ongoing conflict.

Women and men alike had to adapt quickly to the evolving demands of the war, whether it was adjusting strategies on the battlefield, managing medical crises, or delivering critical information under duress. Their resilience is showcased in how they adapted to these challenges and continued to perform their duties effectively.

Stories of Bravery; Captain (Dr.) Seema Rao: know as India's first woman commando trainer, Captain Rao has trained over 20,000 soldiers in close quarters battle and unarmed combat, directly contributing to the readiness and effectiveness of Indian Forces during the Kargil conflict.

" In the face of adversity, it's the spirit and determination that makes the difference."

As pilot in the Indian Air force, Gunjan Saxena and Srividya Rajan where among the first woman to fly in combat zone, conducting evacuation and reconnaissance missions under intense enemy fire.

"It's wasn't just about breaking barriers; it was about proving that women good perform under the same pressure and condition as men."

They few over 40 mission during the Kargil War, providing critical support and saving countless life.

Medical and nursing staff: women in medical rolls like Major Madhuri Kanitkar, played pivotal roles in treating wounded Soldiers, often under direct enemy fire. Major Madhuri Kanitkar said **"There were movements when the line between life and death was razor thin and the Resilience of our medical teams was what made the difference."**

Women in India have served in the military since the 19th century, primarily in nursing roles. The Military Nursing Service was formally established in 1888.Expanded Roles: Women started being inducted into various non-medical branches of the Indian Army in 1992 as Short Service

Commission (SSC) officers. Permanent Commission: In 2020, the Supreme Court of India granted women the right to Permanent Commission (PC) in all ten branches of the Army where Short Service Commission for women was applicable.

Notable contribution:

Some notable women who have made history in the Indian Armed Forces include:

Gertrude Alice Ram was the first female major general of the Indian Army.

Mitali Madhumita: The first woman officer in the Indian Army to receive a gallantry award (Sena Medal) for actions in a counter-insurgency operation.

Punita Arora: The first woman to hold the rank of Lieutenant General in the Indian Armed Forces, and the first woman Vice Admiral in the Indian Navy.

Padmavathy Bandopadhyay: The first woman Air Marshal in the Indian Air Force.

The Kargil was a pivotal movement not only in military history but also in the journey towards gender equality in India. The stories of courage and resilience exhibited by women during the corn flakes serve as powerful remainder of what can be achieved when determination and bravery know no bounds. As we honor their contributions, letters also be inspired to continue breaking barriers and fostering a more inclusive and equitable society.

"IN TRIBUTE TO THE UNYIELDING SPIRIT"

The chapter could end with a reflective note,

Perhaps a personal commentary on how these stories have shaped your understanding of courage and resilience. You might also include a call to action, encouraging readers to support and recognize the contributions of women in all fields.

This structure should provide a comprehensive and compelling narrative for your final chapter, celebrating the courage and resilience of the women who played vital roles during the Kargil War. As we close the pages of "Gallant Women: Stories from Kargil," we reflect on the remarkable tapestry of courage and resilience woven by the individuals who shaped the Kargil War.

This conflict was more than a strategic military engagement; it was a profound demonstration of the human spirit's capacity to confront fear and adversity head-on.From the valor of soldiers in the heat of battle to the unwavering dedication of medical personnel, pilots, and journalists, each story in this book serves as a testament to the indomitable will that defined this pivotal moment in history. The women who broke barriers and stood shoulder to shoulder with their male

Counterparts exemplify a spirit of resilience that continues to inspire and uplift. *General Bipin Rawat* aptly encapsulated this sentiment: "*The Kargil War was a testament to the indomitable spirit of our soldiers and the unyielding support of our nation.*" It is this very spirit that we honor as we look back on their extraordinary contributions. Their bravery and sacrifices have left an enduring legacy, not only in the annals of military history but also in the hearts of those who are inspired by their stories.

As we close this book, let us carry forward the lessons of courage and resilience, embracing these values in our own lives and striving to honor their memory by embodying the unyielding spirit they so beautifully exemplified. The stories of these gallant women and men are a reminder that with unwavering courage and steadfast resilience, we can overcome any challenge and pave the way for a brighter, more inclusive future.